YSAYE M. BARNWELL

NO MIRRORS IN MY NANA'S HOUSE

Paintings by

SYNTHIA SAINT JAMES

HARCOURT BRACE & COMPANY

San Diego   New York   London

Library of Congress Cataloging-in-Publication Data
Barnwell, Ysaye M.
No mirrors in my Nana's house/Ysaye M. Barnwell; illustrated by Synthia Saint James.—1st ed.
p.   cm.
Summary: A girl discovers the beauty in herself by looking into her Nana's eyes.
ISBN 0-15-201825-5
[1. Self-perception—Fiction.   2. Grandmothers—Fiction.   3. Afro-Americans—Fiction.]
I. Saint James, Synthia, ill.   II. Title.
PZ7.B26885No   1998
[E]—dc21   97-33356

E F D

Printed in Singapore

The illustrations in this book were done in acrylic paints on canvas.
The display type was set in Xavier Sans.
The text type was set in Neue Neuland.
Color separations by United Graphic Pte Ltd, Singapore
Printed and bound by Tien Wah Press, Singapore
This book was printed on totally chlorine-free Nymolla Matte Art paper.
Production supervision by Stanley Redfern and Ginger Boyer
Designed by Linda Lockowitz

To Shelvie A. L. McCoy, who grew up in a house without mirrors
and shared her stories and friendship with me, and to our African ancestors,
who understood the wisdom of not having mirrors in the house
—Y. M. B.

For Cousin Rose
—S. S. J.

The author would like to acknowledge and thank David Rousseve, the choreographer who inspired
the song suite containing "No Mirrors in My Nana's House," and Dance Alloy, which commissioned the work;
Sweet Honey In The Rock, who lovingly recorded the song and continues to perform it; Glo Coalson, who
was committed to the life of "No Mirrors in My Nana's House" as a children's book and thus called it into being;
and her editor, Diane D'Andrade, who made it a reality. Finally, she wishes to thank Wanda Montgomery who,
by exhibiting the work of Synthia Saint James and producing Sweet Honey In The Rock in concert in
Charlotte, North Carolina, began the friendship that led to this collaboration. In her passing,
Wanda surely became the guardian angel of this project.

So the beauty that I saw in everything
the beauty in everything
was in her eyes
like the rising of the sun

There were no mirrors in my Nana's house
no mirrors in my Nana's house
so I never knew that my skin was too black
I never knew that my nose was too flat

I never knew that my clothes didn't fit
I never knew there were things that I missed

'Cause the beauty in everything
was in her eyes
like the rising of the sun

There were no mirrors in my Nana's house
no mirrors in my Nana's house

I was intrigued by the cracks in the wall

I tasted with joy the dust that would fall

The noise in the hallway was music to me

The trash and the rubbish just cushioned my feet

And the beauty in everything
was in her eyes
like the rising of the sun
was in her eyes

There were no mirrors in my Nana's house
no mirrors in my Nana's house

The world outside was a magical place

I only knew love and I never knew hate

And the beauty in everything
was in her eyes
like the rising of the sun

Chil' look deep into my eyes

Chil' look deep into my eyes

Chil' look deep into my eyes